When a hurricane blew through the swampy Everglades, two little eggs were swept from their nests and floated down the river. After the storm was over, the eggs hatched side by side in the soft, sweet grass of the riverbank. And that is how an alligator named Spike and a snowy egret named Mike came to live together as brothers in a very special place known as Cypress Glade.

Playing by the Rules

By MARY PACKARD

Illustrations based on characters created
and designed by Lisa McCue

GROLIER ENTERPRISES INC.
DANBURY, CONNECTICUT

One beautiful fall day, Spike the alligator and Mike the bird were picking sugarberries. Suddenly two little birds they had never seen before landed on a bush right beside them.

"Hi, we're jays," said one of the birds. "I'm Jill, and this is my brother, Jasper."

"It's nice to meet you," said the alligator. "I'm Spike, and this is Mike."

"Where are you from?" Mike asked the visitors.

"Up north," replied Jasper. "We're looking for a place to spend the winter."

"Hey, why don't you stay right here?" suggested Mike.

The little birds flitted from one bush to another, checking out their new surroundings.

"It's pretty quiet here," Jill said to her brother.

"At least it's warm," replied Jasper, turning his face up to the sun. "Let's stay for a while."

"You won't be sorry," said Mike excitedly. "Cypress Glade is a great place."

"And wait until you taste these berries!" said Spike. "Would you like to help us pick some?"

Jill popped a juicy sugarberry into her mouth. "Sure!" she replied. "They're delicious!"

"I have an idea," said Jill. "Let's have a contest to see who can pick the most sugarberries!"

"I don't think that's such a good idea," said Spike. "The rule in Cypress Glade is to take only what you need."

"Shh," whispered Mike. "Don't spoil the jays' fun. We want them to like it here, don't we?"

So the four friends picked berries for a long time, even though Spike and Mike knew they were breaking an important rule. Just when their baskets were full, Tallulah came by.

"What are you going to do with so many sugar-berries?" the wise, old turtle asked. "There won't be any more until spring, you know."

"We'll think of something," said Spike, nervously. "I guess we got a little carried away."

Jill and Jasper helped haul the sugarberries to Spike and Mike's house. On the way the jays talked about their summer home up north.

"The city is a wonderful place to live," said Jasper, "but the winters are hard. Sometimes frozen rain called snow falls from the sky and covers everything with a cold, white blanket."

Jill shivered just thinking about it. "That's why we fly south for the winter," she added.

"Why do you go back?" questioned Mike.

"We go back because it's our home, and there's no place like it in spring and summer," said Jasper. "We go to puppet shows, and movies, and concerts in the park."

"Doesn't it get boring here in the swamp?" asked Jill. "I mean, what do you guys do for fun?"

Mike was beginning to feel insulted. "We make our own fun," he said, ruffling his feathers.

That night, before going to bed, Spike and Mike talked about the jays.

"The city may be nice," said Spike, "but I'll bet they don't have sugarberries there."

"Or vine swings, or Spanish moss, or water lilies, or . . ."

"Let's face it," said Spike. "The jays have a lot to learn about our swamp."

"Tomorrow we'll show them how wonderful Cypress Glade is," said Mike. "I'll bet they'll never want to leave!"

The next morning Spike and Mike took their new friends to play on Dixie Otter's mud slide.

"They probably don't have mud slides in the city," whispered Mike to Spike when they got to Dixie's.

The playful raccoons Sass and Frass had just gone down the slide and were splashing in the water. It was Dixie's turn now.

"I have an idea," cried Jasper. "Let's all go down the slide together."

"It's really not strong enough for that," said Spike. "And besides, our rule is to take turns."

"Shh!" whispered Mike. "Let the jays have fun."

"Be careful!" Dixie called out, as everyone piled on the slide at the same time. But her warning didn't help. The slide soon collapsed under their weight.

"Look what happened to my mud slide!" cried Dixie. "It's as flat as a pancake!"

"Don't worry," said Sass. "We'll help you build another one."

"An even bigger one!" said Frass.

"Tomorrow," said Mike, as he hurried off with Spike and the jays. "Today we are showing Jill and Jasper all the good things in Cypress Glade."

Their next stop was Bo Rabbit's house. After digging alone in his garden all morning, Bo was glad to have company.

"What a great place to play hide-and-seek!" exclaimed Jill, pointing to the garden.

"Hide-and-seek in my garden?" cried Bo. "Our rule is to be careful where we play. You might hurt my plants!"

"Don't worry," said Spike. "We'll be careful."

And the group did try to be careful . . . at first. But they were all having so much fun, they forgot to be gentle with the corn stalks and not to step on the peas. By the end of the game, the garden was ruined. Even the squash was squished!

Spike and Mike hated to leave Bo with a mess. But they wanted to continue showing the jays the swamp. So they quickly replanted some of the plants and told Bo they would be back tomorrow to take care of the rest.

When the four friends got to Blossom the beaver's house, she was happy to see them. Blossom loved Cypress Glade and was glad to show any visitors all her favorite places.

"This is Fiddlesticks Dam," she said, pointing to the dam. "We beavers built it out of logs and sticks. It holds back the river. We've had a lot of rain this year, and if we didn't have a dam, most of Cypress Glade would be under water by now," she added proudly.

Just then Blossom's babies began to fuss.

"They're tired," said Blossom. "Why don't you go for a swim while I put the children down for a nap?"

Blossom went into the house while the others stood admiring the dam.

"Look at all those sticks," said Jasper.

"Yeah, they'd make a terrific raft!" added Jill.

"What are we waiting for?" asked Jasper. "Let's go for a ride."

DANGER: Do Not Play Near the Dam

"I don't think we should fool with the dam!" warned Mike.

"'Stay away from danger' is our biggest rule around here," agreed Spike, pointing to the sign.

"It won't matter if we use a few little sticks," said Jill.

"Well . . . okay," said Mike.

While Spike and Mike watched, the jays took sticks from the dam and tied them together with vines. Soon the group had a sturdy raft.

"Let's try it out!" said Jasper, pushing the raft into the water.

Jill and Jasper hopped on. Spike and Mike followed, and away the four friends went.

"Whee!" cried the jays, as the rushing water carried them down the river.

"This is fun!" cried Mike. "Boats don't usually move this fast in the swamp."

Then, all of a sudden, Mike figured out what was happening. "OH, NO!" he cried. "There must be a leak in the dam!"

"A very big leak!" yelled Spike.

Mike took off like a streak. He flew over every part of Cypress Glade, shouting: "HELP! HELP! Meet us at the dam!"

When Mike got back, Spike, Blossom, and the jays were already working to plug up the leaks. One by one their friends arrived.

"What if the whole dam breaks?" asked Gumbo the frog.

"Then all of our homes will be under water!" cried his brother, Jumbo.

"We'll just have to work together to make sure that doesn't happen," said Blossom.

The team worked fast and hard. With so many workers, all the leaks got fixed, but just in the nick of time.

DANGE
Do Not Pla
Near th

"Whew!" sighed Spike. "That was a close one!"

"It sure was!" agreed Mike. "And it was all your fault," he said, pointing to the jays. "Spike told you about the rule. It was your idea to break it, and that's why we almost had a terrible flood!"

"Our fault?" cried Jasper. "You helped!"

Spike and Mike were very quiet. Finally Mike spoke up: "Jasper is right," he said. "We knew better than to break the rules just to please our friends."

"We got carried away," agreed Spike, "but I think we've learned our lesson."

"It's just that we wanted you to like Cypress Glade," said Spike, turning to the jays.

"We do like Cypress Glade," said Jill. "In fact we'd like to spend all our winters here. If you'll have us, we promise to pay more attention to the rules."

"Yes," agreed Jasper. "And we'll show we can be good neighbors by fixing Bo's garden and Dixie's mud slide."

"Great!" said Mike, with a big smile.

"I just had another good idea," said Jill.

"Uh oh!" said Spike. "What is it this time?"

"Let's use all the sugarberries we picked to make jam for everyone in Cypress Glade!" said Jill.

And that's exactly what they did.

That night everyone went to Spike and Mike's house for a jam-making party. Jill thought it was her best idea ever. All the neighbors in Cypress Glade had to agree. Now the sugarberries would last all winter, and it looked like their friendship with Jill and Jasper would last a lot longer than that!

Let's Talk About It

In the story you just read about following rules, Spike and Mike didn't think about the "taking turns" rule until Dixie's mud slide was ruined. They also forgot to be careful while playing in Bo's garden. And worst of all, they took sticks from Blossom's dam, which almost caused a flood.

Why did Spike, Mike, and their friends forget about following their own rules? They were trying to impress their new friends, the jays. They wanted the jays to love Cypress Glade, so they did things they would not have done on their own.

Sometimes it's easy to forget about following the rules, especially if the friends you are with don't understand why the rules are important. But rules are necessary. They help us behave in a way that keeps us safe and happy, especially when we don't have a lot of time to think about what to do.

It's easier to follow rules when you understand them. The next time you have some quiet time with a parent, grandparent, or teacher, make a list of the rules you follow in a day. If you don't know why you should follow a certain rule, ask the adult to help you figure it out. In the future, if a friend wants you to break one of your rules, you can explain the reason behind the rule and save both of you from getting hurt or into trouble.

WATCH YOUR STEP

DO NOT CROSS

BE CAREFUL

Is Water Heavy?

As Spike and Mike and the jays found out, there is a lot of water behind a dam. Which do you think would make a bigger flood — a hole in the top of the dam or one near the bottom? You can find out by trying this simple experiment.

This is what you'll need:
an empty milk carton
a ball-point pen
running water

Use the pen point to poke two holes in one side of the milk carton, making sure both holes are the same size. Make one hole near the top and one near the bottom of the carton. (See the picture.) Place the carton in the sink and fill it with water. Let the water continue to run into the carton in a steady stream. Watch as the water flows out of the holes. Also, feel the water coming out of the holes by passing your fingers through it. What do you notice?

You can see and feel that the water comes out faster and harder from the bottom hole than from the top hole. That's because water is heavy. Its weight presses on the water at the bottom more than on the water at the top. As a result, the water streams out with more force from the bottom hole.

DO NOT DISTURB